ALSO BY LEE BENNETT HOPKINS:

America at War

Wonderful Words

My America

Spectacular Science

Marvelous Math

Hand in Hand

sharing the seasons

sharing the

seasons A BOOK OF POEMS

SELECTED BY LEE BENNETT HOPKINS ILLUSTRATED BY DAVID DIAZ

MARGARET K. McELDERRY BOOKS
New York   London   Toronto   Sydney

MARGARET K. McELDERRY BOOKS

An imprint of Simon & Schuster Children's Publishing Division

1230 Avenue of the Americas, New York, New York 10020

Compilation copyright © 2010 by Lee Bennett Hopkins

Illustrations copyright © 2010 by David Diaz

All rights reserved, including the right of reproduction in whole or

in part in any form.

MARGARET K. McElderry Books is a trademark of Simon & Schuster, Inc.

For information about special discounts for bulk purchases, please contact

Simon & Schuster Special Sales at 1-866-506-1949 or

business@simonandschuster.com. The Simon & Schuster Speakers Bureau

can bring authors to your live event. For more information or to book an

event, contact the Simon & Schuster Speakers Bureau at 1-866-248-3049

or visit our website at www.simonspeakers.com.

Book design by Debra Sfetsios

The text for this book is set in Bernhard Modern Std.

The illustrations for this book are rendered in mixed media.

Manufactured in China

10 9 8 7 6 5 4 3 2 1

Library of Congress Cataloging-in-Publication Data

Sharing the seasons : a book of poems / selected by Lee Bennett Hopkins ;

illustrated by David Diaz. — 1st ed.

p. cm.

Includes index.

ISBN 978-1-4169-0210-2 (hardcover)

1. Seasons—Juvenile poetry. 2. Children's poetry, American.

I. Hopkins, Lee Bennett. II. Diaz, David, ill.

PS595.S42S48 2010

811.008'033—dc22

2009019297

For Charles—
"*always*—
always—"
—L. B. H.

For David and Sindy Durham
—D. D.

contents

SPRING

SUMMER

AUTUMN

WINTER

Spring

"Spring in the world!
    And all things are made new!"

Henry Wadsworth
Longfellow

Spring
Lee Bennett Hopkins

Roots
sprouts
buds
flowers

always—
always—
cloud-bursting showers

rhymes
April fools
fledglings on wing

no thing
is
newer
or
fresher
than
spring.

Swing
Fran Haraway

It's too soon for the front porch swing.
No crocuses are opening.
The wind is from the north and chill.
No matter. Spring is here. I still
Am bound to sit and swing out there
And feel it in the evening air.
It's much too cold. The trees are lean
And leafless—not a sign of green.
It's foolishness to sit outside.
The mockingbird has testified
To spring's existence, and I see
That buds are on the almond tree.
I'm sure it's spring. How do you know?
I think a cricket told me so.

Map to Spring
Rebecca Kai Dotlich

Go straight to Seed,
turn right on Bud,
around a bend to Breeze until
you cross over Puddle: next is Hill.
Turn at Crocus, watch for Wing,
follow New Blossom
to corner of First
       and Spring.

Spring Sun
Elizabeth Upton

I warm chilly bones of winter
melt snow banks
send ice floes gushing.

I open buds on branches,
stir frozen dirt,
release crocus
from its earthy bed.

When I shine
fiddleheads unfurl
their green frills to spring.

Children throw down their jackets,
jump rope, scoot scooters and
call through open air
like new robins.

Don't You Dare
Beverly McLoughland

Stop! cried Robin,
Don't you dare begin it!
Another tweety rhyme
With a redbreast in it.

Another cheery verse
With a cherry tree,
Don't you dare
Write another spring poem about me!

Take your pad and pencil
To the reedy bog.
When you feel a poem coming—
Think: Frog.

Polliwog
Candace Pearson

You don't look
much like a frog,
polliwog,
        darting
backandforth,
        backandforth,
in the shallows,

smaller than the end
of my little finger,
no croak in you yet,
but plenty of . . . . . . spriiing,
as if I'm shooting
rubber bands underwater.

Soon we'll both
grow big, you'll ribbit
right out of this river,
        no longer polliwog,
to take your place
on the bank
fully frog.

Suddenly Green

James Hayford

So suddenly green
Our whole outdoor scene:

It's happened so fast
We're already grassed;

Our trees have grown skin
And birds have moved in.

What strikes me this spring
Is the speed of the thing.

Budding Scholars
April Halprin Wayland

Welcome, Flowers.
Write your name on a name tag.
Find a seat.

Raise your leaf if you've taken a class here before.
Let's go around the room.
Call out your colors.

I see someone's petal has fallen—
please pick it up and put it in your desk
where it belongs.

Sprinklers at recess,
fertilizer for lunch,
and you may snack on the sun throughout the day.

Excuse me . . .
what's that in your mouth?
A bee?

Did you
bring enough
for everyone?

In Concert
Fran Haraway

Yip
Yap
Squeak
Squeal
Whicker
Bray
Bawl
Bleat
Moo
Mew
Nicker
Neigh
Cheep
Chirr
Trill
Tweet
Warble
Sing.

Make a joyful noise—

It's s p r i n g!

13

April Is a Dog's Dream
Marilyn Singer

april is a dog's dream
the soft grass is growing
the sweet breeze is blowing
the air all full of singing feels just right
so no excuses now
we're going to the park
to chase and charge and chew
and I will make you see
what spring is all about

Birthday
Candace Pearson

First,
an egg
sheltered by leaf
warms in spring sun.
Asleep inside,
something dreams
slithery dreams,
long,
straight,
flickering,
mouse-catching
dreams.

Sleep
over,
the shell cracks
from inside out—
a nose,
a mouth,
two half-moon eyes
emerge,
and a newly born
grass snake
uncurls into the
world.

White Wings
Carl Sandburg

Sitting against a big friendly tree
      Reading a book I love,
      I looked up suddenly
And saw fleeting and wheeling
Away in the blue spring sky
      A flock of gray birds
Flashing white wings in the May sun.

Summer

"Summer afternoon—
summer afternoon—
the two most beautiful words
in the English language."

Henry James

Summer
Lee Bennett Hopkins

Fairgrounds
Ferris wheels
cotton candy
h e a t

always—
always—
cool snow cone treats

baseball games
fireworks
mosquito bites

what
surprises
occur
on
long
summer
nights.

Summer Sun
Elizabeth Upton

I warm blue-lipped
lake children lying on rocks
and erase their wet footprints.

I freckle, burn and brown their skin,
grow their bones.

I linger in the evening
so they can
skip, hop, race
play ball
eat Popsicles
and stay up late because
it is too light to sleep.

The Fourth of July Parade

Fran Haraway

Stripes and stars,
Antique cars,
Pretty girls,
Baton twirls,
Spangled gowns,
Friendly clowns,
Smiling folks,
Papered spokes,
Marching feet,
Endless heat,
Clapping hands,
High school bands,
Town traditions,
Politicians,
Perspiration,
Celebration!

Swimming to the Rock
Mary Atkinson

My father and brothers
are swimming to the Rock.
"Come with us!"
they call to me
and I say,
"Maybe next year."

The Rock is very, very far away.

I sit on the dock
with my peanut butter sandwich.
I watch them
dive into the water
and swim into the distance
their kicks and
splashes and elbows
getting smaller and smaller
as they near the Rock.

It takes them a long, long time.

They arrive and pull themselves to stand
and wave their arms in the air.
I can't see it but I know their hands are in fists.
I can't hear it but I know they are cheering.
Even the loons call to celebrate their arrival!

I sit on my dock
dangling my feet in the water
counting dragonflies.

My father and brothers
come closer
and from the water
lift their faces with
wild wet smiles.
And I think

This year!

Sand Castle
Constance Andrea Keremes

Sandra built a castle out of sand.
Eddie, Juan, and Winnie lent a hand.
Winnie scooped out sand to make a moat.
In it Eddie placed a seashell boat.
Sandra built two turrets strong and tall,
Juan pressed pearl-white stones around each wall.
The children spoke of damsels and of knights,
And snow-white steeds and fiery dragon fights.
They sat and dreamed that sunny summer day
Till high tide came and took their dreams away.

Summer Moon
Ann Rousseau Smith

Above the beach,
The summer moon
Follows, like
A huge balloon.

Round and full,
It drifts ahead
As if to say
"Don't go to bed . . .
       Not yet.

Let's play a game
of tug-of-war
Or maybe tag
Along the shore.

My face is full,
Feel free to leap.
The air is warm,
Don't go to sleep . . .
       Just yet."

August Heat

Anonymous

In August, when days are hot,
I like to find a shady spot,
And hardly move a single bit—

And sit—
    And sit—
       And sit—
          And sit!

Summer Storm's Plea
Rebecca Kai Dotlich

Let this downpour be good,
strong, one that frightens frogs,
pounds gardens, rooftops.

Let this be a visit like no other.
One that quakes,
shakes the yapping dog,
the lazy cat, one that comes
bullying, rain-wrapped
in sheets of fury.

Let this downpour be good,
proud as a prank, one wild raid
of rain that drums my name:

Thunderstorm.

Indigo Sky
Candace Pearson

Crickets write a summer night
with long, jazzy notes
scratched against indigo sky.
Their song slices through clouds,
seesaws off the rising moon,
bounces back from stars.

Loud, louder, loudest
still they play
until no one stays asleep.
Spider, fox, mouse and mole
crawl from their beds to listen
and watch fireflies light the show.

Small Homes
Carl Sandburg

The green bug sleeps in the white lily ear.
The red bug sleeps in the white magnolia.
Shiny wings, you are choosers of color.
You have taken your summer bungalows wisely.

Wildflowers
Amy Ludwig VanDerwater

You think the meadow's quiet
at night when you're asleep.
Those lovely summer flowers
simply practice smelling sweet.

Not so.

Trumpet Creeper blows a trumpet.
Glory toots a horn.
Phlox pulls out his pink trombone
and jams until the morn.

Lily waves his stamens.
Rosie swings her skirt.
Daisy wonders who she loves.
Daisy is a flirt.

Violet plays viola.
Thistles strum guitars.
Summer flowers sway and swirl
under August stars.

Cattails tap on tree trunks.
Black-eyed Susans croon.
Dandelion changes costumes
underneath the moon.

Poppy shakes maracas.
Confetti petals fall.
Teasel plays marimba
as Ivy climbs a wall.

Milkweed lets her hair down.
Bluebells ring and ring.
Flowers jump out of their roots
to hear Snapdragon sing.

But when they see the moon set,
each flower takes its place.
Each bloom stands tall upon its stem,
all ready for your vase.

Don't mistake the summer meadow
for something sweet and mild.
Sometimes something beautiful
is hiding something wild!

The Day After Labor Day
Joan Bransfield Graham

September breeze, an island chill,
the streets so quiet . . . still,
    seem wider now
but soon they fill
         with gulls

that stride and squawk
and boldly walk
    the middle of the road—
I wish I understood
         gull-talk

perhaps they, too, feel harmony
no crowds, no noise
    now once again
just sand, waves, sky, and sea
      . . . just gulls and me

Autumn

"Autumn, the year's last,
loveliest smile."

William Cullen Bryant

Autumn
Lee Bennett Hopkins

Pumpkins
frost
longer shirt sleeves

always—
always—
miles of piles of leaves

tricks
treats
geese flocking through air

autumn's
many
marvels
to
share.

After
Prince Redcloud

Leaves
    f
       a
         l
        l
leaf after leaf after leaf after
leaf after leaf after leaf after
leaf after leaf after leaf after
leaf after leaf after leaf . . .

in
quiet

disbelief

Apple Pockets
Amy Ludwig VanDerwater

This morning I have apples in my pockets.
I feel them round and ready and remember
That every year for years (with apple pockets)
The people walk this orchard in September.

A hundred years ago they picked these apples
Small children skipping on their way to school
Young families coming home from Sunday church
Old lovers holding warm hands in the cool.

And when I walk alone I sometimes see them
With apples in their pockets and their skirts.
And when I'm quiet sometimes I can hear them
With merry laughs and boot-scuffs in the dirt.

I reach for an apple and I twist it.
I bite into the white and taste September.
This morning I have apples in my pockets.
I feel them round and ready and remember.

The Scarecrow Prince
Terry Webb Harshman

A scarecrow stands
    among the corn;
his hair is wild,
    his pants are torn,
and on his head,
    a hat quite worn—
crumpled, faded,
    and forlorn.

But when the sun
    shines down on him,
his golden hair
    and friendly grin,
it seems to me
    a prince is born—

Royal Keeper of
    the Corn.

Bewitched by Autumn
Rebecca Kai Dotlich

My favorite time of year. Here,
in a city carved with candlelight,
a whistling in the air tonight
of toad song, porch stoop,
swish of broom
in a sweep of sky.

One brew of wind, and I
am flying in this autumn-mood
of apple breeze, fall moon, star spell.
My days are full with point of hat,
branch of wand, curl of silver
chimney smoke,

bits of legend in a broth,
steamed with a spot
of bubble and spice, full
of hoot and cider and singing wind . . .

these are magic hours
of chill and cobweb days,
for all too soon, blue star
and winter moon
shall snap them all away.

The Pumpkin Tide
Richard Brautigan

I saw thousands of pumpkins last night
come floating in on the tide,
bumping up against the rocks and
rolling up on the beaches;
it must be Halloween in the sea.

When
Craig Crist-Evans

Our house smells
like pie,
roast turkey,
stuffing,
peas,
candied sweet potatoes,
jellied cranberries,
apple cider,
ham,
bread,
mashed potatoes,
gravy . . .

Gramma and the rest
of the family
all came for
Thanksgiving feast.

48

Everybody's smiling,
talking,
remembering
last year,
telling stories,
hugging,
shaking hands,
watching football,
and wandering about . . .

there's so much noise
I have to stand on a chair and shout . . .

When do we eat?

For Crows and Jays
Beverly McLoughland

I sing a song
Of thanks and praise
For cranky crows
And feisty jays
Who could have lived
A life of ease
Sailing on a southern breeze
But gave up warm and
Sunny skies
To stay behind and
Criticize
November's damp
And bitter cold—
With squawk, and
Bellyache, and
Scold.

Horse in Pasture
James Hayford

All fall the farm horse at the bars
Just stands, not watching the passing cars,
Not moving his eyes across the view,
Not even—unlike the cattle—feeding.
Poor horse, I say; nothing to do,
Like knitting or whittling, rocking, reading.

November

Florence B. Spilger

End of autumn.
The hop of a wild rabbit
Scuttling through leaves.

Closing Sale
Beverly McLoughland

Autumn's going out of business
Due to threat of snow—
Goldenrod and aster
Chrysanthemum must go.

Bumblebee's out browsing
Nectar's almost gone,
It's Autumn's final bargain days
With Winter coming on.

First Snow in November

Joseph Bruchac

When I see tracks
in the Freezing Moon
they make me want to follow.

The familiar green
of the grass is gone
and where there was a humdrum lawn
a map of white
the sky has placed
is filled with new trails to be traced.

The thump of
Rabbit's double print,
Old Fox's straight line trot a hint
of mysteries that have been sent,
a thousand stories evident—
right there outside my window.

It's time for me to go.

Winter

"...winter tames man, woman and beast."

William Shakespeare

Winter
Lee Bennett Hopkins

Snowballs
snow people
icicles
frost

always—
always—
a mitten or two lost

scarves
boots
earmuffs
sleighs

and
books
to curl up with
on
long
wintry
days.

Boardwalk in Winter
Joan Bransfield Graham

No summer
smells,
and not a
sound,
winter quiet
all around,
boarded-up,
deserted,
bare,
swept by cold
and salty air
the ocean's
roar
is all that's
loud,
an echo of
last summer's
crowd.

Season
Lillian M. Fisher

First snow
falling.
Wild geese
calling.
Fields are
bare.
Winter
whispers
everywhere.

61

FROM

Moon, Have You Met My Mother?
Karla Kuskin

I am softer
and colder
and whiter than you.
And I can do something
that you cannot do.
I can make
anything
beautiful:
warehouses
train tracks
an old fence
cement.
I can make anything
everything
beautiful.
What I touch,
where I blow,
even a dump filled with garbage
looks lovely
after I've fallen there.
I am the snow.

Hidden in Winter

Ann Wagner

Outside of my window,
past snow piled on the sill,
there's a bright swatch of sunlight
on a smooth, snowy hill.

Can't tell where the steps were.
Can't tell flower beds from paths,
and no sign of the basin
where the birds take their baths.

But just past the oak tree
where the sun hits straight on,
there's a small patch of brownness
that might be the lawn,

where six quail are pecking
and scratching about—
they're helping the garden
to melt its way out.

Alone in Winter
J. Patrick Lewis

Have you come upon a doe,
   alone in winter?
I did once. She was shy.
Wind galloped through the trees
And the trees stepped back
And the doe made a slow
circle in the air
with her wet black nose,
as if to say,
I have come upon a boy,
   alone in winter.

Icicles
Lee Bennett Hopkins

Swell
and
grow,

put on
your
mighty show

this
bitter-bold,
brutal-cold,
howling,
windy-wintry
day—

'cause
you
cannot
know
tomorrow's
tad
of sunshine prey

will
stalk

to
take

your
breath
away.

Swan
Lee Bennett Hopkins

Frozen pond. Thick ice.
A tough, harsh winter test for
Swan awaiting spring.

Winter Home
Rebecca Kai Dotlich

We build our beds
inside this barn,
with shreds of cloth,
old rags, twine. A room
where we can winter-dine
to chime of ice, by windows full
of snowflake art. With dreams of crumb,
cracker, tart, inside this old
wind-whistling place, this cold
and tiny mousekin space,
we cuddle to chase
the chill away,
imagining an April day.

And Then
Prince Redcloud

I was reading
a poem
about snow

when
the sun
came out
and
melted it.

Cat
Marilyn Singer

I prefer
warm fur,
a perfect fire
to lie beside,
a cozy lap
where I can nap,
an empty chair
when she's not there.
I want heat
   on my feet
    on my nose
     on my hide.
No cat I remember
dislikes December
   inside.

December
Sanderson Vanderbilt

A little boy stood on the corner
And shoveled bits of dirty, soggy snow
Into the sewer—
With a jagged piece of tin.

He was helping spring come.

Acknowledgments

THANKS ARE DUE TO THE FOLLOWING FOR PERMISSION TO REPRINT THE SELECTIONS BELOW.

❋ Mary Atkinson for "Swimming to the Rock." Used by permission of the author, who controls all rights.

❋ Joseph Bruchac for "First Snow in November." Used by permission of the author, who controls all rights.

❋ Craig Crist-Evans for "When." Used by permission of the author, who controls all rights.

❋ Curtis Brown Ltd. for "Bewitched by Autumn," "Map to Spring," "Summer Storm's Plea," "Winter Home" by Rebecca Kai Dotlich, all © 2010 by Rebecca Kai Dotlich; "Autumn," "Spring," "Summer," "Swan," "Winter" by Lee Bennett Hopkins, all © 2010 by Lee Bennett Hopkins; "Icicles" by Lee Bennett Hopkins, which first appeared in *Once Upon Ice,* selected by Jane Yolen, published by Boyds Mills Press, © 1995 by Lee Bennett Hopkins; "Birthday," "Indigo Sky," "Polliwog" by Candace Pearson, all © 2010 by Candace Pearson; "After" by Prince Redcloud, © 2010 by Prince Redcloud; "And Then" by Prince Redcloud, which first appeared in *Good Books, Good Times!* selected by Lee Bennett Hopkins, published by HarperCollins, © 1990 by Prince Redcloud, and all reprinted by permission of Curtis Brown Ltd.

❋ Lillian M. Fisher for "Season." Used by permission of the author, who controls all rights.

❋ Joan Bransfield Graham for "Boardwalk in Winter" and "The Day After Labor Day." Used by permission of the author, who controls all rights.

❋ Fran Haraway for "The Fourth of July Parade," "In Concert," and "Swing." Used by permission of the author, who controls all rights.

❋ Harcourt Inc. for "Small Homes" from *Good Morning, America* by Carl Sandburg, © 1928 and renewed 1956 by Carl Sandburg; "White Wings" from *Breathing Tokens* by Carl Sandburg, © 1978 by Maurice C. Greenbaum and Frank M. Parker, Trustees of the Sandburg Family Trust, and Harcourt Inc. Both reprinted by permission of Harcourt Inc.

❋ Terry Webb Harshman for "The Scarecrow Prince." Used by permission of the author, who controls all rights.

❋ Helen Hayford for "Horse in Pasture" from *Star in the Shed Window: Collected Poems* by James Hayford, ©1962 by James Hayford, and "Suddenly Green" from *Notes Left Behind: Last and Selected Poems* by James Hayford, © 1997 by James Hayford.

❋ Constance Andrea Keremes for "Sand Castle." Used by permission of the author, who controls all rights.

❋ Sarah Lazin Books for "The Pumpkin Tide" from *The Pill Versus The Springhill Mine Disaster* by Richard Brautigan. © 1968 by Richard Brautigan. Used with the permission of Sarah Lazin Books.

❋ J. Patrick Lewis for "Alone in Winter." Used by permission of the author, who controls all rights.

❋ Beverly McLoughland for "Closing Sale," which originally appeared in *Cricket,* November 1998; "Don't You Dare" and "For Crows and Jays," which originally appeared in *Cricket,* November 2000. All used by permission of the author, who controls all rights.

❋ Marilyn Singer for "April Is a Dog's Dream" and "Cat." Used by permission of the author, who controls all rights.

❋ Ann Rousseau Smith for "Summer Moon." Used by permission of the author, who controls all rights.

❋ Scott Treimel for text of "I am softer / and colder" from *Any Me I Want to Be* by Karla Kuskin. © 1972 by Karla Kuskin. Reprinted by permission of Scott Treimel NY.

❋ Elizabeth Upton for "Spring Sun" and "Summer Sun." Used by permission of the author, who controls all rights.

❋ Amy Ludwig VanDerwater for "Apple Pockets" and "Wildflowers." Used by permission of the author, who controls all rights.

❋ Ann Wagner for "Hidden in Winter." Used by permission of the author, who controls all rights.

❋ April Halprin Wayland for "Budding Scholars." Used by permission of the author, who controls all rights.

Index of Titles

INDEX OF AUTHORS

Index of First Lines

About the Author

LEE BENNETT HOPKINS is a distinguished poet, writer, and anthologist whose poetry collections include the highly acclaimed *Hand in Hand: An American History Through Poetry*, illustrated by Peter M. Fiore, and *My America: A Poetry Atlas of the United States* and *America at War*, both illustrated by Stephen Alcorn. Mr. Hopkins's numerous awards include the University of Southern Mississippi Medallion for "lasting contributions to children's literature," both the Christopher Award and a Golden Kite Honor for his verse novel *Been to Yesterdays: Poems of a Life*, and the NCTE Award for Excellence in Poetry for Children. He lives in Cape Coral, Florida.

About the Illustrator

DAVID DIAZ has been an illustrator and graphic designer for more than twenty-five years. His bold, stylized work has appeared in editorials for national publications such as the *New York Times*, the *Washington Post*, *Business Week*, and the *Atlantic Monthly*. His children's book illustration work has earned him many honors and awards, including the Caldecott Medal for *Smoky Night* by Eve Bunting. He has also illustrated Newbery Honor book *The Wanderer* by Sharon Creech, *The Gospel Cinderella* by Joyce Carol Thomas, *Counting Ovejas* by Sarah Weeks, and *The Little Scarecrow Boy* by Margaret Wise Brown, which was named a *New York Times* Best Illustrated Book. Mr. Diaz lives in Carlsbad, California.